THE MENTOR 3 - COMPLETE INFLUENCE

Cuckoldress Supremacy

ALLORA SINCLAIR

Cuckoo
Publishing

THE MENTOR 3 - COMPLETE INFLUENCE

Front Cover Illustration by: Ufabizphoto

Joshua and Kim, I still remember the first time we met at "the resort". This book is for you. I'll never forget the time when we... oops. I almost forgot. What happened there, stays there. Hugs and Kisses to both you wonderful people.

CHAPTER ONE

*I*t had been a full week since Anna and her princess were at Julia's with the four bulls and an additional week since she first put the cock cage on her husband. It amazed her at how quickly he recovered from his emotional meltdowns. Julia kept insisting Anna leave the cage on, so her cuckold would recover quicker. She was right.

Today, Anna decided it was finally time to reward her little baby princess. He had been such a good boy. He deserved to have some sexual pleasure for her to feel less than a horrible human being. She consulted with her mentor before she did anything silly.

"Good afternoon, Miss Julia. How is my lovely today?" Anna had now picked up the lingo of talking like an elite segment of the population.

"Hello, my love. I'm just stupendous. How's your little princess managing?" Julia responded.

"Funny you should ask. That's actually why I'm calling."

"Oh, really. Is the poor little princess having a hard time bathing his little self?" Both women spoke of their husbands like they were their children, rather than their husbands.

"No. I'm thinking of letting him out of his cage so he can... Um, you know," Anna said in a playful voice.

Julia snickered. "Well, Miss Anna, I think that's acceptable, but you need to be careful in what and how you do things here." She said with authority.

"I know. I know. Cage on as soon as he blows?"

"No. What I mean is you still need to make him understand you are his Goddess. What the princess may get from his Goddess has changed forever. Keep that in his mind and he should recover with no grief."

"Go on." Anna needed a more explicit set of instructions from her mentor.

Julia elaborated on what Anna was to do and what she should avoid. Anyone listening in to the conversation would have been embarrassed at the crass nature both women were now completely comfortable talking in.

Anna hung up the phone and she felt she was making the right decision. She wanted to make her princess have his fun in the quickest and easiest way she could. Now that she was no longer working, she had all the time in the world to plan and execute any plan her heart desired.

Anna shaved her legs, and pussy like she was seeing a bull. She knew her husband had a pantyhose fetish, so she put on the pair with the perfect shade and silkiness she knew would drive him nuts, making sure not to have any panties on underneath. She also knew he loved her more when she looked like a bad girl. She applied her make-up to accentuate the look. She had now gone back to full-time smoking in the house, so she knew this would also help elevate his excitement. As Miss Julia instructed, Anna wanted to give her princess the illusion that he was finally going to get a chance to fuck his wife on his terms.

When the princess arrived home from work, Anna greeted him at the door, looking for a way that would push all his buttons instantly.

"Uh, hello?" He said, almost stunned at the sexual energy his wife was throwing his way.

"Hello? That's all you have for me? How 'bout 'Good afternoon, my beautiful Goddess. You look amazing'?" Anna said.

"Well, hell ya! You looking fucking amazing. Please don't torture me. This cage hurts when I get hard and you're making me hurt right now."

Anna wasted no time, taking his hand and leading him up to their bedroom.

"You see this?" She dangled the key to his cock cage, looped around her neck

He nodded, having a look of pleading desperation on his face.

"Today is your reward day. I want to reward you for being such a good little princess. Would you like me to take the cage off and reward you?" Anna teasing the obvious.

She removed the key from her necklace and intention-ally pretended to struggle with the lock. He was growing by the second as she continued to move the cage around, having 'so much difficulty that maybe she should just forget it'. The lock clicked open, followed by an enormous sigh from her husband, knowing he would finally enjoy a full orgasm.

"Okay, little princess. I don't want to touch that dirty, nasty little thing until you freshen him up. Let's go to the sink and bathe this poor little boy." She was comfortable and unapologetic in speaking to her husband like he was a little girl.

Almost running to the bathroom, he turned the water on and strained to hang his cock over the sink, isolated, so he could apply soap and wash without the water pouring down his legs. Anna stood behind him, looking at him in the mirror.

Her once strong and dominating husband, she realized, had changed so much. Now he was her bitch. A helpless little puppet. She had total control over every single string attached to him. He willingly was self-deprecating and looked ludicrous. The power she had over this man was infinite. The more she had, the more she wanted. With every passing day, Anna could feel her insides craving more. While he dried off, she realized her Goddess status was indeed a seductively addictive and wonderful place that she would now protect and defend, at all costs.

"There ya go. Oh my, you are a good little princess, aren't you?" She said, feeling the rush of adrenaline as she embraced her darkest side.

He turned, grabbing her by the neck, wanting to ravish every inch of her body. His mouth craving her lips, her neck, her tits. He wanted all of her, but he was lost with desperation.

Her hands moved as her newly manicured nails gently scratched on the way down. His body thrust against her side, his cock poking like a desperate puppy scraping the door, wanting entry from the outside cold. Her hand wrapped around his hard cock. She stroked it only enough to make him shudder.

Anna then pushed him onto the bed, spread her legs, and straddled his face. He was consumed with desire. This would be the payback. He would finally have his wife to himself. It convinced him he had enough sexual energy to fuck her over and over. She continued to shift, immersing him in the heavenly scents of her pussy.

She turned around to see his cock was now a flag pole.

"Oh look, your cock is hard. But it looks even smaller now that you've been wearing a cage for so long. Let me look at it closer."

Anna got up from sitting on his face and walked around to the bottom of the bed. She had one of her pantyhose covered legs straddle his chest so he could feel the nylon with his hands. She then bent over and softly put his cock in her mouth. She made every motion soft and gentle, intentionally trying to keep the sensations at a minimum.

The princess squirmed for more. He thrust his pelvis in an attempt to go deeper into her mouth. Anna recoiled, sat up, and put both of her hands on her waist.

"What do you think you're doing? You don't get to move like that. Like you're a... a real man." She said with a disgusted face.

"Oh please, Anna. I mean, my Goddess. I'm sorry. Please."

The longer he suffered, the more fun she was having. She considered putting his cage back on but decided he should have a release this time. Anna took the bottle of lubricant by their bedside, applied a liberal amount, and began stroking his cock.

"My Goddess, I would like to fuck you. Please may I fuck you?"

Anna smiled, remained silent, and slowly increased her up and down movements. His cock throbbed. She could tell he was trying to withhold himself from exploding, but he was so wound up. She stroked even more aggressively.

"Please Anna, please. I don't want to... to....t..."

Anna was sure to show no mercy. She was relentless in stroking him harder and harder.

"Oh, my little baby princess. Your cock is so fucking pathetic. I love you, but that thing you call a dick will never see the inside of me, ever again. It's what we both want. You want me to fuck other guys only. It turns out, so do I." She said this with such a sadistic tone, being sure she timed it at the perfect moment where he could no longer delay the inevitable.

He erupted, firing cum in every direction. Just missing Anna's face, the balance landed in various parts of the bedsheets and on his chest. Anna waited for nothing. She got up, grabbed a towel, and walked back into the room.

"Ok, princess. Wipe that shit of yourself and then I need the bedsheets cleaned. I can't sleep in that."

"But I I..."

"I I what?" She demanded. "Do as your Goddess tells you. Then go have a shower quickly, so I can put your cage back on your..." she paused for dramatic effect. "Back on your teenie tiny little princess dick. GO!"

CHAPTER TWO

hree days elapsed, and the princess remained in a depressive state. Anna, for the first time in weeks, felt remorseful. Had she been too cruel to her husband, not allowing him access to her body? Despite Julia's reassurance that he would snap back, it did not seem to happen. Her instinct was to forget the whole cuckol-dress thing and go back to vanilla. This was too painful for her husband, who at her heart, she loved deeply. Each day was met by a man that looked and acted broken. Anna knew him well enough to know he was hating himself.

Sitting on the couch, watching one of her new mid-day soaps, the phone rang. It was Julia doing her daily 'check-up' on her newest protege.

"Hello, my love. How's your little princess? Has he finally realized?"

"Julia, I'm glad you called. I'm sitting here thinking. I

know you and I have gone back and forth a million times with this, but I don't think I can do this anymore."

There was a long pause before Julia responded.

"Miss Anna, I'm coming over. You live in the Tapscott area, no?"

"Yes, but I don't think that will be necessary. I'm going to tell Robert when he arrives home that we need to stop this. I feel like I'm destroying him."

"Enough. Give me your address, and I'll be there in about an hour."

Anna reluctantly gave the address and then went to freshen up for visitors. Knowing Julia, she could see her bringing some bull with her. Though she would love to have some real fun and get rid of all her stress, she was hoping Julia would come alone. She put on some make-up, made a fresh pot of coffee, and had a cigarette while she waited.

"Miss Anna, look at you. You're breathtaking, even with track pants and a sweatshirt," Julia said as she entered the house.

"Thanks, Julia," Anna looked out the front door to make sure she came alone.

"What a lovely house you have here. I take it your princess is hard at work?" Julia emphasized the word 'hard,' as she spoke.

"Actually, no. He's a mess, and so am I, if I'm to be honest," Anna said.

The small talk extended into the kitchen where Julia made herself at home and poured herself a coffee. Prompting Anna to join her at the kitchen table, she lit a cigarette without asking and offered one to Anna. She reluctantly accepted.

"Miss Anna, I think what we have here is a situation where you and your husband are about to enter the last stage of cuckoldry. Just like the four stages of grief, denial, anger, bargaining, and acceptance, the old you as a couple is dying."

"But Julia, I'm not bargaining here. I just want this roller coaster to end."

"Oh, really? So tell me a small part of you didn't kinda hope I brought a powerful, young man over with me, to fuck your brains out? Tell me, Anna."

Anna's face went red as her eyes darted in every direction but Julia.

"Wellllll…"

"Well, what? You love this lifestyle. There is no way you would have lasted this long without it fulfilling a part of who you are. It feels right to you. And I'm telling you, it feels right for your princess."

"But Julia, why has he been so depressed and unresponsive to me and our family since I got him off. I mean, I put his cage right back on afterward, but he never seemed to bounce back."

Julia nodded.

"I get it, Anna. Been there, done that. Your little bobbies, I mean princess, has realized his life belongs as your cuckold. He wants it badly. He actually needs it. All he's doing now is bargaining with himself for some kind of internal resolution."

Another long pause as both women outed their smokes. Anna smiled. A small part of her knew her teacher and mentor was spot on.

"So what do I do? I feel so guilty seeing him hurt this much," Anna said.

"Well, Miss Anna, consider yourself extremely lucky to have me in your life. I know the perfect solution that will end this, once and for all."

"Do tell." Anna squirmed in her seat with excitement. She did not want this fairytale to end. Julia was right. This was her. She passed the point of bargaining when those four men had their way with her. She was already in acceptance. But her husband was not.

"Three words, my love. The Cornuto Resort," Julia did not wait for Anna to ask.

"It's a sort of cuckold training facility. A boot camp, if you will."

"Seriously? You want me to send Robert, I mean my princess to a boot camp?"

"No, silly girl. It's a resort, my love."

"Okay, where? How? What?"

Julia smiled, watching as Anna's face beamed with excitement and curiosity.

"Relax, Miss Anna. Relax. I must check with fluffy, to see if we can fit it into our schedule. It's a remote tropical island resort, nestled off the coast of Jamaica. We land at Sangster International in Montego Bay. Then we have to take a hydroplane boat ride to the island. It's quite nice."

Anna got up and paced the kitchen floor as she pushed for more information.

"So what is it? I'm lost, Julia."

"Calm down, girl. This resort has been around for over 20 years. I heard about it when fluffy and I were new to cuckolding. Try to imagine your wildest dreams, then times them by 10. This place will fix everything for you as a couple. When you get home, your little princess won't ever have the ability to go back to vanilla anything. Actually, neither will you. It's a wonderful place," Julia had never looked more sexy and seductive to Anna. This woman was her personal savior.

Julia called her cucky to see if he would want another trip to paradise. He was on board and booking the trip for the four of them before she could hang up the phone.

"Fluffy's looking into it now. He's gonna book the time off if he can get us all reservations. We can make it a foursome. Oh, Anna, you're going to love this place."

"But what about my princess? What if he can't get the time off work, and what do I tell him? The truth?" Anna was barely touching the floor as she danced around imagining the possibilities.

"Anna, you talk like your princess has a say in the matter. My love, you own him. Tell him you feel the need to have a couple's vacation somewhere far away from here. That's all he needs to know."

"Do I tell him you and fluffy will join?" Julia thought it was cute how Anna spoke to her like she was her mother.

"Na, we can surprise him at the airport. In the meantime, you, my love, need to go shopping for ridiculously expensive swim and clubwear. Let's make it a girls' day out."

"Oh. Oh. Let's get our hair done too." Anna had already forgotten all concerns she had over her husband.

"Great idea, Miss Anna. Tomorrow, I'm booking us both in for a day at the spa as well. A nice massage, manicure, pedicure, waxing. We'll be looking fine for our vacay." Both women giggled devilishly.

CHAPTER THREE

*P*rincess arrived home to an empty house. After settling in, he started the dinner preparations, following the notes Anna had left on the counter. She entered a few moments later as a thrilled and excited Goddess. Bags in hand and dressed to kill, Anna had not told him anything until that point.

Following Julia's instructions, she accentuated her sexuality to help her little princess oblige without objection.

"Hello, my cute little princess. How was my little girl's day?"

He bashfully looked down at her feet and smiled in appreciation for her candor.

"I I I'm fine. I mean m m my day was f f fine."

"Oh, is my little princess getting all worked up? You are such a cute little girl to your Goddess. You make me so happy. I love you so much."

He wiped his hands clean of the food debris and went to greet her with a kiss. Anna could see he was slowly coming back to his normal self. His cuckold self. The self she loved and wanted to keep forever.

"I have some wonderful news for my princess. You've seemed a little down in the dumps, the past couple of days, so I've decided we are going on a vacation together."

He looked confused and concerned.

"You mean just me and you? The two of us?" He asked.

"Yes, my princess. The flight is already booked, so tomorrow, you need to schedule next week off. We leave in two days. Look, I've already started getting some sexy outfits." She pulled the bags up from the ground and started removing thong bathing suits and clubwear that would make anyone in the vanilla world embarrassed.

"Oh, my goodness. This is delightful, my Goddess. You are so good to me. Thank you for doing this. I think this will be great for both of us, don't you?"

"Oh, my little princess. You do not know how much we both need this." Anna said with a note of something more.

"And, and, and, it's just you and me, right?" He wanted to be sure he was not misreading her.

"No bulls are coming. I promise you, we will have more fun than you could imagine." Again, Anna said things with a hint of something else.

Dinner was soon served and discussion of the tropical island paradise dominated the conversation. The princess became increasingly attentive to every whim of Anna's as she continued to taunt him with innuendos of humiliation, Anna could see that Julia was once again correct. Her husband was at his core, a cuckold. He loved her as his Goddess. She loved herself as a Goddess. It cemented her conviction to make this trip a success when she went off Julia's script and told her cucky that Julia and fluffy would join them.

"Oh, your wonderful friend Julia is coming?" He asked, with a solid idea that the ramifications of the trip would likely be more convoluted than first presented.

"So you don't mind? Fluffy will also join to keep you company."

Her princess smiled from ear to ear. He understood what was in between the lines now. He seemed to appreciate Anna returning to her more forceful and God-like attitude. She could see he was rapidly returning to the much happier and compliant little princess she needed him to be. If she could just keep him in this headspace all the time... Anna went to bed dreaming of life post-vacation. She could see things being so magical. Julia had helped her see what a beautiful life she was missing. It almost made her wet thinking about it.

She felt wet. The daylight bounced into the room as Anna turned to an empty space beside her. She had fallen asleep and slept well past noon before rising. Checking her phone, she had a single text from Julia and her princess.

From her husband;

MY GODDESS, I LOVE YOU. THE BOSS HAS GIVEN ME THE WEEK OFF.

And from Julia;

GOOD MORNING MISS ANNA. TONIGHT. HOTEL 6 OFF STERLING DR.

BRADLEY WANTS YOU AGAIN. YES OR NO?

Anna took just enough time to let her eyes focus before responding.

HELL YES! SOLO OR YOU'RE JOINING?

She hit send, considering nothing other than what was she going to wear.

Two cups of coffee and four cigarettes later, Anna realized her princess did not know she was going out to play on her own. This would be a first for the couple. She had reached a point where she no longer cared if it upset him. The trip will fix this if it becomes a problem, she thought to herself. She will endure another day or two of cry baby behavior if he responded negatively. Leaving before he arrived home, she left a note on the front hall table.

GOING OUT TO PLAY. SHOULD BE HOME BY AROUND NINE THIRTY? I'LL SAVE THE CLEAN UP TO YOU. TODDLES XO G.

Although she was feeling apprehensive on the drive there, the extended moments of euphoria, satisfaction, and release made her forget she was also a mom and a wife. There was no foreplay, no wine and dine. In, get it on, and get out. She was back on the road and heading home early.

"I'm home," Anna yelled as she came in from the garage door.

Her princess bounded down the stairs, eager to greet her with no wasted time.

"Hello, my Goddess. I hope you had a wonderful time. How can I be of service?"

Both of them knew what he wanted. An opportunity to bury his face in between her legs while the scent was still fresh. Anna knew how she handled herself in this situation would be critical for the following several days.

"Oh, look at my lovely little princess all excited about eating my pussy, after a real man has paid a visit. Oh, that's just adorable."

He was visibly shaking with excited anticipation. This

was the payoff. The proper reward for being such a good princess, he thought. Anna pulled out a cigarette, prolonged her lighting ritual, and blew the full extent of exhaled smoke into his little baby girl lungs. He coughed as she laughed at his softness.

"You, my little princess, have been a bad little girl the past few days. I think you should think about what you did and think hard. I'm tired and need my beauty sleep. You can have your cage removed when we get upstairs, but I'm going to bed. You can play with your little dick by yourself."

It filled his face with glee. Just knowing he could whack off was enough. He needed to blow and his wife was allowing him this privilege, which was merciful in his mind.

"Thank you, my Goddess. Thank you." He said with sincerity.

"Tomorrow, I'll be out all day. Julia and I have appointments for hair, nails, massage, and something called Reiki. I won't be home for dinner, so make sure you pack your bags. Mine is already done." Anna said like a drill sergeant.

"So we leave on Saturday? What time?" He asked.

"Flight is at 8 am so you must be up early enough to make me a nice breakfast and go downtown to pick up Julia and fluffy. I'll be ready to leave by 6 am when you return with them. Okay, my little baby princess. Happy hand job, baby. Love you."

CHAPTER FOUR

*B*oth couples left Anna's house as scheduled at 6 am. All occupants of the car remained quiet for the entire drive. It was too early for the women. Their pampered lives had shifted early to mean 10 am. Princess and fluffy sat up front making minimal awkward small talk around the traffic conditions, best routes to the airport, and the weather. Princess was told to hail a porter, and they instructed fluffy to purchase coffees for both ladies while the two women stood at the entrance doors, enjoying their last cigarettes before boarding the flight.

At check-in, Julia reserved two individual seats immediately next to the washrooms. Anna and herself sat together in first class where they would be treated accordingly. The 5 and a half hour flight across two time zones placed them in Montego Bay just before lunch, local time. The tropical smells jumped into the cabin the moment they cracked the plane doors open. Paradise was just around the corner.

"Come on, fluffy. I want to check out the local cuisine," Julia made sure she said this with enough volume that every passenger within 500 feet could hear.

"Yes, dear. Coming dear" was his meek response.

"Why doesn't he call you Goddess?" Anna asked.

"Oh that. I don't want to feel embarrassed in public," Julia making the double standard her point.

Outside of the airport arrivals, a sea of cabs and tour buses awaited new guests to the country. Each tour operator stood with a sign stating which operator they represented. A tall, muscular and extremely attractive black man in an Armani suit held "CORNUTO" against a clipboard. They were home.

"Hello, you sexy man. I haven't seen you in over a year. How's your brother?" Julia asked.

"I'm fine, thank you, Miss Julia. Raymond is looking forward to seeing you again. And how's your fluffy doing?" The driver spoke to the couple like they had a long history. "And who is this lovely lady you've brought with you?" He took Anna's hand and kissed it like she was royalty.

"I'm Miss Anna. And this is my little princess," she pointed to her husband with little regard.

The driver laughed at the name creativity the two women had developed for their cuckold husbands.

"Well, hello princess. Welcome. I see this is your first visit here at the resort, although, I'm sure it won't be your last. All the ladies love it here and the men... they learn new things about themselves every time. Again, welcome." The driver looked like he was native to the country, but spoke with no accent. He sounded well educated from an Ivy League school.

"So Miss Julia, we've changed our resort location since

your last visit. It's now on the main island. Towards Negril, off near a little town called Black River."

"How long of a drive from here?" Julia asked

"It's about three hours. Don't worry. We'll take good care of you ladies. Good care indeed." He said smiling as he loaded the women's luggage onto the coach bus that looked decked out for a rock star.

"Um, excuse me s s ,sir." Princess trying to get the man's attention. "What about our luggage?"

The driver gave him a blank look and pointed to a beat-up diesel van from the late 80s that sat behind.

"Your Goddess will travel with me. If you hurry, you and fluffy can follow behind. Sorry for the lack of seats. Just use your bags to sit on. Oh, and be sure to roll the windows down. Come on, ladies. Let's get this party started. Champagne?" He said to both women as they went to board the coach bus. The door opened exposing a strong pungent odor of cannabis and loud club music. They tinted the windows dark, revealing nothing except a few silhouettes that looked like male bodybuilders.

Princess could feel his cock hurting from the cage confinement as he and fluffy jumped into the sweltering van. No driver. No seats. No air conditioning. This was what every good cuckold deserved, he thought to himself. As long as they treated his wife like a Goddess, he was a happy, lucky man.

The entryway to the resort was obscure and miles away from any form of civilization. The perimeter gates were guarded by a team of security personal that ensured entry and exit were always controlled. An additional ten minutes of road weaving its way deep into a tropical jungle finally opened to a structure that looked more like a castle than a resort. Surrounded by massive green space, the land-scaping was immaculate.

Awaiting their arrival at the grand entrance stood 5 young men, all shirtless, all delicious eye candy for the ladies. Princess and fluffy pulled up in sweat-stained shirts and a strong taste of gas in their mouths. The exhaust system in their vehicle was less than effective in venting all the fumes.

"Hey, guys. How was the drive for you?" Julia approached the van.

"It was wonderful, my Goddess. Thank you for allowing me to join you on this trip." It was the first full sentence princess had heard fluffy speak to his wife since meeting him.

Anna came forward, now wearing one of her thong bikini's recently purchased.

"How ya doin my little princess baby girl?" She leaned in to kiss her husband.

Princess could taste a powerful combination of tobacco, weed, and alcohol when they kissed. His Goddess was already well on the way to incoherence.

"I I I I'm fine. You look w w wonderful, my Goddess. D D Did you have a g g good time on the b b bus?"

Both women laughed uncontrollably.

"Let's just say, I was fully briefed on how this trip is going down. I'm so so so excited for you, baby. You are going to thank me so much, so… you're welcome in advance." Anna struggled to avoid slurring her words.

"Okay ladies, the boys have taken your luggage to your rooms. Your cuck's will need to come with me for their orientation assessment and designations. My name is Jerome. You're free to enjoy the pool, the bar, the beach.

We'll let you know when you can see them again so say your goodbyes please." A new face said this. An extremely tall and handsome caucasian in his mid-forties. His Armani suit matched that of the drivers.

Julia kissed her index finger and then placed it on fluffy's lips. Winked and walked away with no words being said.

Anna was so far down the rabbit hole of feeling no pain, she did not know whether to kiss, hug or copy her mentor.

"What's happing Anna... I mean, my Goddess? I thought this was to be a vacation for both of us. I'm not understanding. What's going on here?"

"Ooooh, baby princess. You're just such a cutie pie. You'll be fine. I can't wait to see what they do to you." Anna said without restraint.

Scared, confused, and unsure of what was about to happen, princess knew at that moment that his wife, Anna, had finally crossed over. No matter what the future had in store, the woman he married was no longer. This woman was a significant improvement. It was the woman he had always wanted in his heart. She was a Goddess in every way imaginable.

"Okay girls, follow me. And make sure you take your bags with you." Jerome said to both husbands.

CHAPTER FIVE

They took both men down a long hall with dismal lighting and no windows. It led to an elevator that looked more like it was more for service than for guests. Princess noticed nothing specifically odd about the resort until several men walked past them wearing female panties.

"Is this place a resort or a prison?" He asked fluffy.

"Oh, it's a resort all right. I love it now."

"What do you mean, 'now'?"

"You'll see," was fluffy's only response.

As they entered the elevator, the princess could not help feeling like the men with them were more security personal rather than concierge staff.

"Where are we going and why is the elevator going down?" Princess regretted trusting his partner in crime.

"Just you relax, missy. We's gonna take good care of you's."

The elevator continued its journey down several levels below ground. Was this a James Bond thing? Princess could not help thinking as fear developed.

The doors opened to a reception area with an attractive female receptionist sitting behind the counter. She stood up, showing off her model figure, and extended her hand.

"You must be the princess. Welcome." She smiled, revealing perfectly straight white teeth and a tan most women would kill for. "And is that you fluffy? I haven't seen you in over a year. Where have you been and why haven't you come to visit me until now?" She said with playfulness in her baby talk voice.

"Come this way, ladies."

Princess couldn't help noticing that every person they met since arriving was referring to them like they were females. It was cool that his wife degraded him, but he was unsure how he felt about the public being let in on their little secret.

There was no sunlight. No decorations. Once they passed reception, she led them down into an area that more closely resembled a hospital hallway. Each room's door closed. Stark white walls and no furniture.

"Okay, it was all fun and games lady, but where the fuck are you taking me?" He could no longer stay in cuck mode. He felt his personal safety was being compromised.

"Shhh. If Jerome hears you, you'll be in huge trouble. Just relax and let us do our job." The receptionist said as she escorted them into a room with two steel chairs, a white desk, and over 20 TV monitors on the wall behind.

"Jerome will be in to see you in a moment. Would you like water?" She asked before leaving.

Both men declined as the man that greeted them outside passed by her and entered the room. He came behind princess and put a firm hand on his shoulder.

"Princess, I have two things to tell you before we get started. Number one, don't fight it anymore. Number two, learn to embrace and crave it." He smiled and then went behind the desk to sit in a luxurious leather chair facing them.

"Fluffy, you've been here so many times I think I've lost count. Do you need anything or did you want to join your Goddess?"

Fluffy smiled and gently asked if he could have his cage removed and have his special room just for the evening.

"Absolutely. I completely understand." Jerome leaned forward, hit a few keystrokes with his laptop on the desk and the door behind them opened with a man waiting to escort fluffy to 'his room'.

"So princess, I guess this leaves just the two of us. Questions before I begin my brief presentation?"

"Um, ya, one. Am I free to leave cause I feel this is like a prison?"

Jerome leaned back, placing both hands behind his head, and smiled.

"No princess. You are no longer part of the world as you know it. Your wife has signed a waiver declaring you violent, mentally unstable, and a threat to her safety. Ya, know, just in case you ever decide to come after us legally. Either way, you belong to me and my staff until we deem you safe for reentry into society. So no, you are not free to go."

"What the fuck!? Okay, this is just getting too weird, even for my... thing."

"Relax, princess. No one's going to hurt you or anything. This is a behavioral modification facility that helps little cucky's like yourself make the last shift. We're here to help you, not hurt you." Jerome sounded articulate and sincere with his words.

"But what if I don't need help or want it?" Princess remained confused and concerned for his well being.

"Princess, let me explain something." Jerome went to his computer, clicked a few keys causing all the monitors behind him to light up with live video feeds to every square inch of the resort, including all the bathrooms.

He continued.

"That little thing around your tiny dick, your cage. That's supposed to be entertainment for your Goddess. As it stands right now, it's being used for you, to help you control your emotional waves." He allowed princess to speak, which he did not.

"When you are done here, you will be a proud cuckold. You will not be ashamed of who and what you are. You will not need that cage to help keep you in check. Would you like that, princess? Would you like to be cage free and still be a cuck?"

His eyes widened with any thought of freedom being utopian.

"So what exactly are you going to do with me then?" Princess said with irritation.

"Well, the professional names are cognitive behavior therapy and operant conditioning. To you, all you need to know is we are going to break you down to the smallest common denominator and then we are going to rebuild you so we complete this last piece of being a cuckold. It's very simple. Our success rate is 100%"

Princess jarred when the statistic was revealed.

"100%? You mean when I get out of here, I'm going to be a cuckold and feel good about myself? Okay, that's the first thing you've said that I like. If this is what I need to do, I'm in." Princess shifted his temperament, knowing the endgame was not punishment but help.

"I'm glad to hear you're on board. Let's see what Anna is up to now." Jerome went back to the laptop and pulled up 6 cameras, all watching his wife from various angles.

"Each of our Goddesses wears a tracking bracelet so we can find them instantly. So here we have Anna making out with three of our hired bulls. Did she tell you she was going to do this or is she cheating on you?" He asked as he looked back to princess for a response.

"She did not tell me. I just assumed she was going to do some flirting while I went to our room. She's only kissing them, anyway. It's not like she's having sex." Princess said defensively.

"Oh? Let's look at the recorded footage on the bus ride over here."

Jerome pulled up other video feeds with Anna and Julia clearly on the bus. He could see both women ingesting several kinds of narcotics, sucking the cocks of all 5 men on the bus, and then being shared in a gang bang spit roast. As princess watched, he could not keep his hands above his groan. He wanted to masturbate as he watched his wife get pummeled by all 5 throughout the hot, sweaty drive he suffered in the van that followed.

"Here, princess. Here's the key. I'm going to leave you to watch the whole thing in private. I'll be back in an hour to see if you're still on board."

CHAPTER SIX

*J*erome returned two hours later to find Robert hunched over and convulsing. He approached and placed his hand on his back.

"I know, princess. I know. Believe it or not, I understand." Jerome trying to console his newest guest/patient.

"H H How can you under under understand?" Princess turned to face him, his eyes were bloodshot with tears streaming down his face.

"Princess, right now you're grieving. You're recognizing that a part of you is dying inside. The man you have pretended to be to everyone, including yourself, is not the man you are. But, it's the man you think you should be. Why? Why continue to put yourself through this? You are a cuckold. You can not get enough of Miss Anna as your Goddess. You have always been a cuckold. You even want to be a cuckold. You were happy and excited when I told you earlier that we can help you remain a cuckold for the rest of your life. You want this, I know you do. Please sit up and let me help you."

Princess's crying subsided with the comfort this man was offering. His heart was so conflicted. If Anna only knew what she was putting him through, she would stop this. They could go back to their normal vanilla life.

"Please. Come with me. Let's get you settled in your room. It's just darling." Jerome made sure he delivered his words with flamboyant patronization.

His room had pastel pink everywhere. The walls had a floral pattern, and the carpet was Snow White. It reminded the princess of his daughter's bedroom when she was a little girl.

Built into the wall was a huge 64 inch TV that dominated. The bed was a small single with light purple silk sheets and covered with a white duvet sporting a violet pattern in random locations. On the night table was a full box of tissue and a reading light.

"Do you like your new home, princess? Isn't it just groovy?" Again, Jerome with his pretend flamboyancy.

"Where's my suitcase with all my clothes?" Princess asked.

Jerome smiled and pulled open the drawers against the opposite wall. One drawer had female panties, another had women's tank tops and shorts. Nothing would fit, at least to size.

"What's this? I want my clothes. This is all women's clothes."

"I know. Don't worry. You will have lots of clothes to wear once you stop fighting yourself. Now, come sit down on your bed. I've arranged for Anna to be interviewed shortly. She does not know you will watch this, so enjoy."

Jerome turned the TV on. The image looked like it was a live feed to a seating area on the beach. The sound of crashing waves subtle in the background. A swimming status flag blowing proudly on the main beach in the distance.

"I do not know what you're going to hear, princess, but it might be worth remembering this. We will make sure we make a copy of this interview available at the front check-out when you and your Goddess leave. That way, you can always revisit it at home if you ever forget how she feels." Jerome's words sounded cold, but his demeanor seemed genuine and concerned as he left the room.

A few moments went by when an extremely attractive woman appeared to walk into the video feed and sit down with her back to the camera. Seconds later, Anna walked into the shot and sat down facing the hidden camera.

"Hi, Anna. I'm not sure if you remember meeting me earlier today at the party? My name is Candice. Are you enjoying your stay here at the resort?"

Anna could not contain herself with joy. She nodded as she laughed.

"Oh, my fucking God. This place is fucking amazing. I'm loving this shit!" Anna responded.

"Good, I'm glad to hear. So anyway, we always interview all our Goddesses as a sort of customer service and control. Ya know, to see if we can make any improvements for future guests or your return. We're interested more in your current relationship with your husband and how this cuck camp may help. Do you mind if I ask you some personal questions"

"Go right ahead. Anything I can do to make the next time back here even better, I'm in."

"Great. So first I want to ask you about your husband's reason for coming. Did he know what he was getting into?"

"Um, not a clue," Anna responded.

"Did you know what we were all about? The training that we will place your husband through?"

"Hell ya! I can't wait!"

"I see. And how long have you and your husband been in this lifestyle?"

Anna thought back. It seemed like a long time, but in actuality, extremely short.

"About 2-3 weeks... I think. I don't know. It's been such a whirlwind of fun that I've lost track of time. I'm sorry."

"It's okay, Anna. So tell me, what's your thoughts about being a cuckoldress, or a Goddess as most of the cuck's call their wives?"

"I LOVE IT. LOVE IT! I wish I'd known my princess was a cuck ten years ago when we first got hooked up. Ten years I missed. Oh well, this week I plan to make up for all the lost time if ya know what I mean." Anna said.

Candice laughed in understanding.

"Remember, you still must walk when you get back home." She offered as a girl to girl joke.

"Now, tell me about your husband."

"Who? Oh, you mean my princess? Sorry, I've almost forgotten he's also my husband."

"Yes, that's right. How do you feel about your princess being a cuckold through and through? Do you like the idea of him submitting to you as your cuckold? Tell me what's your thoughts."

Princess sat on his bed watching the interview unfold with bated breath. He was happy to see his wife live and enjoying herself. Up till now, her responses did not bother or please him. This was the question that held his undivided attention.

"Robert, that's my princess's actual name. He's um... useless in the bedroom. He's a great guy. A decent father and a good man. But I always wanted that and more. I wanted a stable guy that could provide for me and my kids. However, I did not want a guy that took me for granted, had zero bad boy spirit, and a soft dick smaller than my pinky. This cuckolding thing... now, I get it all. AND, princess seems to be so much more attentive and loving and the icing on the cake, he's into it too. Oh, I just love it."

"I see. So, are you saying you would like us to help you do whatever it takes, even if it seems cruel or mean, to help push your princess into being a cuckold for the rest of his life?" Candice asked, being sure to pause for emphasis on each point she raised.

"YES, YES, YES AND DOUBLE FUCKING YES! I love him dearly. I will always love him and want to be with him forever. But do I want him to just give up fighting and jump on the cuckold train with me? Fucking right, I do. You guys are doing amazing things here. You do whatever you need to do. You bring him back to me as a full cuck, I'm coming back for sure." Anna was still a little under the influence. Her willingness to be wordy apparent.

"Okay. So how would you feel if the princess does not respond well to our therapy? Will this affect your marriage, going forward?" Candice asked.

"Look, I know princess is a cuckold. He knows it. I know I love being a cuckoldress. I love EVERYTHING about it. I just hate when he keeps going back and forth about the whole thing. Believe me, you will have no prob's. If he is still the same, then I guess I'll go back to being a boring wife and... Look, I don't even want to think that way. Just tell him I want to fuck other guys and I like to control him. He knows he loves that about me. Ya know what's funny?" Anna stopped to light a cigarette and take a sip of her wine before continuing. "So do I!"

This was the most loving and amazing words out of his wife's lips since he heard "I do." Princess felt like he was truly the luckiest man in the world to hear his wife say everything except that she would be willing to go back to a boring housewife. His cage had still not been reinstalled. His dick was rock hard as he pleased himself into oblivion for the next minute. Cleaning himself off, he wanted out. This place was nuts. He wanted to go home. They had locked his door as he heard the interview restart from the beginning.

Sitting on his bed, he began to cry. Anna was such an amazing wife and princess found himself loving her even more for saying what she did. He was crying because he felt ashamed that he wanted the same things as his wife. He did not want his wife to be anything but his Goddess. He would watch it again, just in case he missed something'. His dick started growing again when he heard her say she wanted him to become her cuckold forever. She was so amazing.

CHAPTER SEVEN

⚭

our more days of up, down, up, down mental and emotional turbulence plagued princess. They confined him mostly to his room, where constant video feeds were broadcast of his wife's ongoing sexual escapades. They required him to attend individual and group therapy in between marathon masturbation sessions he had in his room.

He was physically exhausted from the hyper-concentrated wave of cuckold angst he felt he would never escape. Each day, he could see his wife was looking happier, healthier, and more resolved in being a Goddess. Her tan was deep and dark while her sexual confidence and needs skyrocketed. He remained pasty white from seeing no sunlight beyond the journey from the airport to the resort. His dick, now developing friction burns from the excessive self-pleasure.

As he attended the group sessions, he sat in a circle of

men, all looking confused and distraught. Each would talk about the constant internal fight they suffered from. The uncontrollable desire they had to want their wives to continue their journey into cuckolding, contrasted with their own need to fight this same desire. Jerome, who princess realized led each session, was a decent man that sincerely wanted to help.

"So, princess, how do you feel today? Do you feel the same as sissyboy over there?" Jerome asked.

"I just want this to end. I want to stop feeling so happy and amazing towards my wife and then feel the crash of hating myself for not being able to be 'the man' she needs and wants."

Jerome paused as several of the men felt connected to princess's words and felt the need to verbally agree with the essence of what he was saying. Once the cross-talk diminished, he continued with his probing.

"Princess, who says you have to be 'the man'? Who? Society? Your mommy? Who?"

"I don't know. I just feel less than a real competent husband. I hate myself for this. I HATE IT and I'm just so tired feeling this way." Princess's eyes started welling up as he dug deep into his soul for words.

"Princess, you are this way because you are who you are. It's not your fault. You are a real man. In fact, you're more of a real man than any of the guys up top. They could not have the strength to go through what you and every other man in this room are going through. They just want to get off and that's all they're good for. You're everything to Miss Anna except the sex. Is there anything wrong with that?" Jerome could see princess was on the verge of a breakthrough. He would soon be ready to join his wife.

"But I don't want to be this way." Princess's lip was trembling

"Maybe not. BUT YOU ARE! And it's not your fault. Let me ask you this. Do you want Miss Anna to be controlling? Do you want her to humiliate you? Make fun of your age discrepancies or your femininity? Do you love that she wants to fuck other men? Do you? DO YOU?" Jerome spoke as if no one else was in the room.

The strain left princess's face. His pouty lips ceased.

"Of course I do. I can't get enough of her when she is that way. She was never that way when we started dating, so I just thought…"

"You just thought what? You thought she had the mean girl streak before you dated and found out she seemed more like a good little girl. So you just accepted her and let your genuine desire to see her cuck you get buried?" Jerome was no longer playing soft and tender with his tone.

"Yes. I suppose that's true." Princess said.

"So, you've always wanted her to be the way she is now?"

"Y Y Yes. I love who she's become. I am the luckiest man in the world."

The group of men all chuckled at the same time. Every man in the room felt the same way about their wives. They all seemed to connect with what princess was sharing.

"Okay, so let me get this straight. You love your wife the way she now is. You've always wanted her to be this way, even before you started dating. You don't want her to go back to the way she was, but you want to be her 'real man'? Does this make any sense to you, princess?"

"I don't. I I I don't know. You You You're confusing me."

"Stop fighting, princess. Stop fighting. Your marriage is perfect. She wants to be the way she is. You want her to be the way she is. She wants you to be her little cucky boy. You love being cuckolded. YOU JUST NEED TO ACCEPT IT'S WHO YOU ARE. Stop fighting yourself. That's all you need to do." Jerome waited for the epiphany to reach princess's consciousness.

"But why do I keep feeling ashamed and hating myself for being this way? Why?"

The group all joined in with the same "ya, why?". This was the common goal that needed resolution for all of them.

"Because it means you will give up one small piece of your manhood forever. And society has trained you to think that's the most important piece of manhood. It is not. Being true to yourself is what's most important. Stop fighting yourself and accept that Miss Anna owns you completely. Once you do that, my work is done here."

Princess went back to his room, recognizing Jerome was right. He loved everything about this new life. He did not want it to go back to the way things were. It was the perfect relationship. His wife fulfilled all his wildest needs and fantasies and by being her cuckold, he was allowing her the same. He turned his TV on to see what his goddess was up to.

CHAPTER EIGHT

*A*nna sat with Julia around an open fire pit. Surrounded by torch lights and about a dozen other women, they settled in a seating area of the beach. To princess, it looked like this was a lady only gathering. Both women looked ravishingly beautiful. This lifestyle did Anna wonders for her self-confidence and happiness. She was glowing as the fire reflected. By the deep blue and tangerine sky, princess assumed the women must be having their post-dinner cocktail and cigarette.

"Julia, I'm worried about my princess. Do you think he's ok?" Anna asked.

"Miss Anna, he'll be fine. I'm more concerned about the big day tomorrow."

"What? Do you mean his graduation ceremony? Or are you talking about the cuckold wedding ceremony afterward?" Anna looked so happy. She was everything princess had ever dreamed of, and more.

"Well, yah. It's a big deal for both of you." Julia tilted her wine glass, staring into Anna's eyes.

"Hah! And I thought you knew me, Miss Julia. I'm not worried at all. At least, not from my end. I know what I need to do. I'm actually very excited about it." Princess could see his wife was no longer on any fence. She had made a full transition into a cuckoldress in every part of her being. She could not have been more attractive in his eyes. This is what he had been looking for his entire life.

"Anna, what if he still fights his old self? What if he's not willing to give everything up? Have you thought about that? I've been here over half a dozen times and I've seen a few meltdowns. It's painful to watch. I just hope you're past the point of... ya know, going back to the way you were." Julia was pushing Anna to say out loud what she needed to be thinking.

"Miss Julia, I'm a Goddess. This resort. The amount of dick. O'm God. I don't think I could go back. I admit it. I am officially addicted to this life. I want more. Don't you worry about me. I'll make things happen. Besides, I miss seeing my little princess. He is such a good man and his little dick is so cute."

Both women burst into laughter so intense, princess swore he heard one of them snort like a pig. Julia seemed to have a hypnotic effect on his wife. Hell, she had a hypnotic effect on him. Reflecting, princess could not remember why he so strongly objected to Julia becoming a close friend of his wife. Perhaps he instinctively knew this woman would bring out what both of them needed and it scared him. Perhaps he felt he didn't deserve to feel this happy.

Happy? Princess was happy? Was that happiness deep

inside? He did not feel empty or alone. No. It was not happiness. His mind reeled to understand why he felt so good. Was he just horny knowing his wife deeply wanted him to embrace being a cuckold? He had just whacked off to Julia and Anna's dialogue, so it couldn't be that. What was he feeling? Using the only means of connecting to the outside world, he pushed the intercom button and asked if he could see Jerome ASAP.

"Hello princess. I was waiting for this. You finally sound at peace. Tell me, what's on your mind." Jerome said over the intercom.

"I I I think I'm done."

"Do tell. What makes you say that, princess?"

"Because I think I have now accepted myself for who I am. And that's okay. I'm okay if I am a cuckold. I'm okay that I like to be humiliated. I'm okay that I love my wife to control and humiliate me. I'M OKAY THAT WE BOTH WANT HER TO FUCK OTHER MEN. I'M OKAY!" Princess's tone and volume increasing as he spoke.

"I'll be down in 5 minutes," Jerome said as the intercom clicked off.

Princess kept repeating the phrase "I'm okay," over and over until the door opened with Jerome. He remained standing as princess sat on his bed rocking back and forth like a little girl.

"Look at you princess. You look like a proud little cuckold. Is that what you are? Are you a proud cuckold?"

"YES! I now understand what you've been trying to do with my head. To reach a point of acceptance. Am I right?" Princess asked, not expecting Jerome to respond.

"You finally get it. Good. I'm so happy for you,

princess. Now, here is a paper your Goddess signed two days ago. I can pull the video feed of her signing it." Jerome passed the paper across.

I, GODDESS ANNA, WANT TO SEE MY PRINCESS (ROBERT) WEARING GIRLY PANTIES. I DO NOT WISH TO SEE HIM UNDER ANY CIRCUMSTANCES UNTIL HE AGREES AND WANTS TO WEAR THE PANTIES BECAUSE IT PLEASES ME. DO NOT LET HIM OUT UNTIL THEN.

Signed HIS GODDESS

Princess smirked, lay the paper on the bed, and walked across to the drawers containing all the women's wear.

"I'm so proud of you, princess. We are finally breaking through." Jerome said like a father to his daughter. He continued.

"We have one more session with you tomorrow morning, but I think this time tomorrow, you'll be ready to celebrate with Miss Anna. You may even have time to get some sun before you leave the following day."

"Thank you, Jerome. Thank you so much. And please thank my Goddess. I can't wait to see her."

"She can't wait to see you either, princess. She can't wait." Jerome shut and locked the door.

CHAPTER NINE

Five days ago, when princess arrived, he could not understand all the men walking around in girls' panties and thongs. Today, he strutted into the group meeting wearing a thong, tank top, and was freshly shaved. The new attendees looked at him like he had five heads. The meeting was welcoming to the newbies and a graduation celebration for one. Princess. He was so happy he could finally stop fighting. The look of envy from some of his peers made him feel compelled to leave with the same words given to him.

"Ladies, when you stop fighting and start accepting, everything becomes marvelous. Trust Jerome, cause he has helped me so much." He then was the first to leave with a celebratory cheer from some members close to the same realization.

When the elevator opened, princess strained to adjust his eyes to the bright, early afternoon sun. Proudly walking down the hallway with his girly outfit, he could feel the anticipation of seeing his Goddess as a new person. A man who was also a very proud, happy, and content cuckold.

Strutting out on to the pool terrace, Anna watched in disbelief. They did it! Her husband was no longer. He was now her cuckold. This was AMAAAAZING! She burst out of the patio chair and ran to him.

"I love you so much, my Goddess. Thank you so much for this trip. I am yours." He said as she approached.

"Oh, look at you. You look so cute in that thong. I'm proud of you. I missed you too. They have a few special things planned for us today. Have you eaten?" Anna asked.

"Yuppy. I had fruit loops and a banana." He responded.

"Great. Well then, let's get started. Have you seen Jerome?"

"I just left him. He should be up here in about an hour. He told me to tell you."

They both went back to the deck table Anna had come from when Julia came out from the building. Her hair, looking like she had had some fun.

"Well, hello there, little princess. I must say, you do look cute in that outfit. I think it's wonderful." Julia said, sitting down.

"Where were you?" Anna asked.

"Oh, you know. I had to see my friend Raymond at least once before we go home. His brother sent him up to our room, and... ya." Julia being her cavalier self.

"So where's your fluffy?" Princess asked.

"He's still upstairs. Cleaning up all the mess we made." Julia looking at the couple with a bonding smile. They needed nothing else.

Two cappuccinos later, they could hear a commotion

stirring inside the grand hall, just inside from the pool area. Furniture screeching, voices ordering directions. Both women looked at each other and smiled. Julia mouthed the words "it's time". Anna gave a gentle nod and lit one last cigarette.

"Come on, baby princess. That's them getting your graduation celebration ready." Anna patted his inner thigh, noticing they had removed his cage.

They all stood up and walked toward the noise. Entering the building, Princess's eyes struggled to see anything. It was darker than he remembered. As his vision adjusted to the reduced light, he could see there were chairs all formed in a circle. In the center were a king-size bed and a love chair. It looked completely out of place in the middle of a lobby.

"My Goddess, what's going on? I'm confused." Princess said, feeling nervous about the unknown.

"Oh, relax princess. You're going to remember today for the rest of your life." Came from Anna's friend Julia.

Slowly people shuffled into the seats. Close to a dozen women sat in the front row and the men dressed in panties filled the outer seats, with and without girly tops.

"Come on baby girl, it's showtime," Anna said as she grabbed his cock and pulled him into the center where the bed and loveseat sat.

She pushed him into the love seat and removed the little clothing she had on. The men clapped as she revealed everything. They played a drum roll on the house speakers as all eyes turned to the princess. No. They were not looking at the princess. They were all looking beyond princess. Someone approached from behind him, tapped his shoulder, and said, "I'm so proud of you princess. "

It was a voice he recognized. Before he could turn around, Jerome walked in front of him and gave him a salute. The man had no clothes on. The man was built. Built like a brick house. Every woman looked on with delightful envy. They all knew they would have their turn with him soon enough.

Now that princess could see this man in broad daylight, he appreciated his natural beauty. Jerome looked like a Greek God. He was the epitome of an Alpha male. His dick was easily eight inches without being hard. Princess could only imagine what it would grow to. And grow it did.

Anna wasted no time. She put Jerome's cock in her hand as they walked together over to princess.

"You see this. This is a real man's cock. Stand up. Show everyone what I've had to deal with for so many years." Anna was completely sober and unimpaired. Her voice was loud and forceful.

Princess stood up. She pulled his thong so hard; it snapped off. She grabbed his cock with her other hand.

"This is fucking pathetic. Look at it. What do you think, ladies?"

All the women started chanting "loser, loser, loser, loser"

This was too much to take in at once. His dick remained soft as Anna stroked Jerome's making their size differential even more.

"Sit down, shut the fuck up and watch your Goddess get fucked by a real God."

She pushed him back into his chair, then dropped. Princess was instantly oblivious to the spectators. His hand was on his cock before her knees hit the ground.

She wasted no time. Jerome's cock was so big, she had to shuffle back before launching his cock into her mouth. Easily 10 inches of man slithered in and out between her lips. Jerome looked at princess and yelled, "Tell me you're grateful. Say thank you, Jerome. SAY IT!"

Princess responded like he was in a church choir chant. With enthusiasm and pride, he thanked Jerome loud and clear.

Jerome placed his two gigantic hands behind Anna's head and drove her mouth towards his cock. She choked. Her gag reflex was exercised many times recently, but this was something very new.

Princess could not stop stroking his own cock. He no longer cared about anyone but his Goddess. She had worked herself into a frenzy, trying to get this supreme bull fully erect. Every part of her body moving with one sole goal in mind. This beautiful man needed to fuck her till she was no longer capable of fucking. She had never been there. Jerome was the man.

The men sitting at the back began standing up to see over the women. Unaware of his surroundings, princess failed to see several women had now spread their legs and were satisfying themselves as they watched the man that would fuck them too.

In a fit of uncontrollable sexuality, princess wanted to see more. He wanted his Goddess to be in a rapture with this gorgeous man. Jerome was wonderful. Without thought, he shouted, "I love you, Anna."

Jerome grabbed a clump of Anna's hair and pulled her head back. The room went silent. Anna looked up to Jerome as a completely submissive woman willing to do anything to please her bull. He shrugged towards princess, looked back to Anna, and asked her, "Did you hear what he called you? He called you Anna!"

"YOU CALLED ME WHAT?" Anna stopped everything, stood up, and walked towards princess. His heart was racing with fear and adrenaline.

"You have crossed a line that I will no longer tolerate. Do. You. Under. Stand? I SAID DO YOU FUCKING UNDERSTAND ME?"

"Y Y Y Y Yes m m m my G G G G God God Goddess." Princess felt like he couldn't breathe.

Anna shook her head in disgust, placed both hands on her hips, and walked back to Jerome. She stood silently, staring at the ground, continuing to shake her head. Finally, she looked up with a complete resolution in her gaze.

"Fine. You caused this to yourself, princess. I am going to end this now. Get your little dick over here." She paused again for dramatic effect, then changed to a seductive and sensual tone. "I have a delightful surprise for you, my little princess."

CHAPTER TEN

*T*he room remained quiet. Princess took baby steps towards his Goddess, using both hands to cover his cock. He had suddenly realized the spectators glaring. He could not make eye contact with anyone remaining focused on the floor in front of him.

"Y Y Yes, my G Goddess?"

Anna firmly grabbed his chin and whipped his head to look in her direction.

"I AM YOUR GODDESS. YOU ARE MY LITTE TEENIE TINY PEE WEE CUCKOLD. YOU WILL ALWAYS BE MY CUCKY. YOU WILL DO ANYTHING AND EVERYTHING I ASK. Isn't that right, baby girl?" Anna strained her hand to force his head up and down, regardless of what he would say.

"Yes, that's right, princess. Now here, give me your hand."

Princess extended his right hand, not understanding what was about to come next.

"Good little girl. Now here, hold this, and hold your own cock and tell me USING YOUR WORDS little girl. Tell me your cock is a joke." Anna had captivated the attention of every person in the room.

She slowly lowered princess's right hand and placed it over Jerome's cock.

Jerome squealed, "Ah, that's cold," to offer some levity to the dark situation unfolding. A few chuckles could be heard from the back.

Anna got up close to princess's ear and spoke in her masterfully sexy voice.

"You like that, don't you princess? You like how his big hard cock feels. Yours is a joke, isn't it?"

Princess nodded when he was suddenly greeted with a firm smack across his face.

"I SAID I WANT TO HEAR YOU SAY IT." Julia was so proud of Anna as she watched her performance.

"My cock is a joke." Princess was slowly breaking. He could feel the last morsel of his old self evaporating.

"Very good. Now, because of you, Jerome is not so hard anymore. My arms are tired. I need you to use your hands. Yes, that's right, little princess. I want you to get him hard so he can fuck me proper,"

Princess could no longer look into his wife's eyes. He was ashamed of what he had become.

"STROKE IT!" Anna screamed.

The women all chanted, "stroke, stroke, stroke, stroke"

Princess could not resist this amazing woman anymore. He began moving his hand back and forth over Jerome's cock. He could feel it getting firmer and larger with every stroke. Anna continued to whisper into his ear.

"You like that, don't you, little princess? Do you like being my little slut boy? My little pussy? Ooooh, look at that." Anna leaned back and shouted to everyone. "My little princess is getting hard while he strokes my bull. Isn't that so cute?"

Every fiber of his being wanted to stop. He wanted to explain to his wife that this other man's cock did not arouse him. It aroused him that his Goddess could be so ruthless, vile, humiliating, and degrading. She was wonderful. His mind stopped caring. If it made her happy, he wanted more. She was the best thing to ever come into his life.

Anna abruptly pushed princess away and pointed for him to return to his chair. She plunged her tongue deep into Jerome's mouth. His hands explored every inch of this sexy woman's body. This was one of the few cuckoldress's that Jerome saw as a pleasure, not a job.

He cradled her entire body in one motion, lowering her to the bed that lay in the middle of the room. Anna did not need any direction. Her legs spread open, her back arched, all in anticipation of his entry. He grabbed the inside of her thighs and licked her clit. Over and over and over. She had enough teasing. She wanted his rod. Pushing his head out from between her legs, she said "fuck me".

Without saying a word, Jerome was only semi-hard. Looking straight at her, his only words were "you know what to do."

Anna sat up, lifted her hand, and curled her index finger back and forth to the princess. He was being asked to approach the bed one more time. He went to kneel between her legs, at which point Jerome smacked him hard on the head.

"Princess, come here," Anna called him to the top of the bed. She slipped her tongue deep into his mouth, swirling it around. Then, pulling back, she looked deep into his eyes.

"Princess, your Goddess needs fucked. He is going soft." She pointed to the foot of the bed where Jerome stood.

"Come, let's do this together. We'll have fun and it would mean so much to me." Her voice was silky soft.

She turned herself around and got on her knees. She looked at princess and again promoted him to come. He knew what she would ask of him went against everything.

"Princess, I am your Goddess. What your Goddess wants, your Goddess gets. I need to see you do this, little girl. I need to know I can get you to do anything. Now move and let's do this together."

Princess slowly moved to the foot of the bed, joining his wife. She had already started when he arrived. She turned to him, held Jerome's cock in her hand.

"Here, princess. Suck his cock. I neeeeeeed you to suck his cock. It will make me so happy to know you're helping me get him hard. It's almost like having sex with you. So here, suck it." She looked at him, her face angelic.

"I I I d d d don't want t t to."

"I know you don't. But I want you to. And that's the only thing that matters, so suck it, baby girl. Suck it real nice."

Princess closed his eyes and sucked.

"Oh, what a good little girl you are for your Goddess."

She said into his ear as Jerome shoveled his dick deeper into the back of his throat.

Anna moved her hand under princess and stroked his cock. It was unsurprisingly rock hard. She had seen enough.

"Okay princess, your Goddess thanks you. Now go back to the couch and watch."

As princess got off the bed, the crowd cheered him on. Thinking how ashamed he was, he could not help feeling proud that he had crossed that last bridge. He was now officially owned.

All the men in the audience dispersed after princess sat down. The front row women were in awe at the male specimen remaining with his Goddess. Jerome relentlessly went deeper and deeper into Miss Anna. He was indeed the local superhero to all the women. Julia sat beside princess to watch.

"You were a good little cuckold, princess. You did Miss Anna proudly. I know what she's feeling right now and believe me, nothing feels any better." Julia said as she got comfortable.

"You mean you've been with Jerome too?" Princess asked naively.

"Oh yes. Many, many times. All the women here have been or will be with him, eventually. He is the supreme Alpha. But no, I mean, she will be feeling so happy about you. You have made her happier than Jerome could ever do."

"How so?"

"Because now Miss Anna knows she can fuck anyone she wants, get you to do whatever she wants, and you'll love her even more if she does." She giggled. "She now knows you both can live the lives you've both always wanted."

Princess turned to Julia.

"Miss Julia, you're wonderful. I'm so glad you came into our lives."

CHAPTER ELEVEN

eather scrambled into the gym with a full minute to spare. She felt fat and frumpy. All the women looked so fit already. 'I mean, what are they doing here? They don't need this class.' She thought to herself.

She grabbed the last yoga mat available towards the back of the room. The music came on blaring with a ridiculously beautiful woman at the front posing as the instructor. Heather could not believe she was doing this. How could she let herself go this far? She was at least 10 pounds overweight. No wonder her husband no longer seemed to be interested in her. He was always too busy with work or sleeping.

She needed to make herself feel better, more confident. Maybe this class would help get her back in shape. The dancing around was way more aggressive than the guide said it would be. This was to be a beginner's class.

She glanced at the clock when she was sure the class would be ending. There was still a full 20 minutes to go. Sweat was pouring out every part of her body. She was losing her breath, which surprised her. She had quit smoking almost six years earlier. This had to be the wrong classroom. Was she the only person suffering this much?

Looking around the room, Heather realized all the women were hurting. Many were in worse shape than herself. Everyone except one. The woman on the mat behind her.

As the class ended, Heather grabbed her towel and dried off the sweat when the woman from behind approached her.

"Hello. I couldn't help but notice you kept turning behind to look at me. Was I making too much noise," the woman said.

Heather felt a little embarrassed at how obvious her glare must have been.

"Oh, no. I just noticed you're the only woman in this class that looks like you've got things together. I don't know, you just look so... happy."

The woman smiled and extended her hand.

"Well, thank you. My name's Anna, what's yours?"

LET ME KNOW WHAT YOU THOUGHT

Thank you so much for your support. Please feel free to send me an email if you have any questions or stories you'd like me to share: cuckoopublishing@gmail.com

Finally, if you could do me a huge favour and rate this book at the retailer you purchased it from. Even better, leave a comment (good or bad). It helps more than you know.

Thanks again.

Hugs and kisses

A. xo

ALSO BY ALLORA SINCLAIR

ABOUT THE AUTHOR

 Allora Sinclair is a happily married 40 year old mom. She and her loving cuckold husband Dave (davie) have been in a cuckold marriage for over seven years and she has now decided to start documenting their journey. If Allora is not found at her computer, or out shopping for a new pair of shoes, she is usually found in the caring arms of davie or embraced in ecstasy with one of her favorite bulls. She has done a series of non-fiction books to help couples navigate their way through the heavily distorted life of being a cuckold couple. She is now working on a series of fiction books that are loosely based on some of their real-life adventures. This story is admittedly a stretch.

www.ingramcontent.com/pod-product-compliance
Lightning Source LLC
Chambersburg PA
CBHW071236170626
46809CB00008BA/3092